Torch Fishing
with the
Sun

Laura E. Williams

Illustrated by
Fabricio Vanden Broeck

Boyds Mills Press

I dedicate this book with love and understanding to the memory of my father, Charles R. Williams. He never knew his grandchildren, but he will influence their lives through the influence he had on mine.
And I send my love across the ocean to my friends in Hawaii. Aloha and Mahalo!
With special thanks to the people at Boyds Mills Press. How can so many nice people all work in one place?

—L. E. W.

For Nadia, Carlo, Fabio, and Alexis

—F. V. B.

Text copyright © 1999 by Laura E. Williams
Illustrations copyright © 1999 by Fabricio Vanden Broeck

Published by Caroline House
Boyds Mills Press, Inc.
A Highlights Company
815 Church Street
Honesdale, Pennsylvania 18431
Printed in China

Publisher Cataloging-in-Publication Data
Williams, Laura E.
Torch fishing with the sun / by Laura E. Williams ; illustrated by
Fabricio Vanden Broeck.—1st edition.
[32]p. : col. ill. ; cm.
Summary: Young Makoa must have faith in the strength of his aging grandfather.
ISBN: 1-56397-685-4
1. Hawaii—Juvenile fiction. 2. Grandfathers—Fiction—Juvenile literature.
3. Fishing—Fiction—Juvenile literature [1. Hawaii—Fiction. 2. Grandfathers—
Fiction. 3. Fishing—Fiction.] I. Vanden Broeck, Fabricio, ill. II. Title.
[E]—dc21 1999 AC CIP
Library of Congress Catalog Card Number 98-72493

First edition, 1999
The text of this book is set in 18-point Tiepolo Book.
The illustrations are done in acrylic.

10 9 8 7 6 5 4 3 2

WHEN I WAS A CHILD, growing up in Kahala, Hawaii, I had a wonderful time exploring the beach that came right up to our backyard. I could hunt for buried treasure, pretend I was lost on a deserted island, and fish to my heart's content. I also very often inspected what other fishermen caught.

One fisherman kept his pink rowboat anchored right off our backyard. He caught squid and let me and my friends touch the tentacles. At high tide, men would stand on the beach in their rubber shoes and catch tons of little silver fish. And on calm nights, dark shadows would wade through the shallow waters, holding burning torches above their heads.

These were the torch fishermen. They moved slowly and quietly over the sand and coral, one hand holding a torch, the other a spear. The fish and squid were attracted to bright lights. In a flash, a fisherman would plunge his spear into the water, catching a meal on the barbed end of his spear.

Although this tale takes place in a fictional land, I used references to Hawaii. For example, the name *Makoa* is a Hawaiian name that means, among other things, "fearless and courageous." *Kimo* is simply Hawaiian for James. A *plumeria* is a flower that smells as sweet as it is beautiful, and it comes in many colors from dark pink to soothing yellow. The type of canoe the Hawaiians used is called an outrigger canoe. It has a pontoon attached on one side, or sometimes on both sides.

—Laura

A long time ago, when the wind had a name and the stars pointed the way, there lived a boy named Makoa. Makoa lived with Grandfather in a small house near the sea.

As soon as Makoa was old enough, he followed Grandfather down to the beach every afternoon and helped him push his small canoe onto the water.

"Where are you going?" he asked, even though he already knew the answer.

"I am going torch fishing with the sun,"
Grandfather said. "If I don't pull the sun from the sky
and make it night, how will the torch fishermen catch
any fish with their feeble flames?"

From the beach, Makoa watched Grandfather paddle his canoe to the far edge of the sea, where he said he caught the sun in his net. Then the sun and the boat slowly slipped over the horizon, and the sky became dark.

Soon the torch fishermen came down to the beach, walking back and forth in the shallow water. They held their torches high to attract fish to their spears. Makoa watched them awhile before going home to sleep.

In the morning, Makoa ran back to the beach and waited impatiently for the mist to clear. Then, in the shell pink dawn, Makoa saw a speck no larger than a grain of sand balancing on the far edge of the sea. As he watched, the speck came closer and closer until it finally looked like a man in his canoe, the paddle skimming the waves. As the canoe came even closer, Makoa could see the man was Grandfather, bringing home a giant fish for them to eat.

One night, after Grandfather had paddled over the edge of the sea with the sun, a boy squatted down next to Makoa and said, "My name is Kimo. Is your father torch fishing?"

"My grandfather is," Makoa said.

"Which one is he?" Kimo asked.

"You cannot see him," Makoa explained. "He is over the edge of the sea, and he uses the sun as his torch."

Kimo threw back his head and laughed. "Oh, I have heard about your grandfather. He is the old man who paddles down shore every night. He gets his fish from one of the neighboring villages."

"That is a lie," Makoa said angrily, standing up. "My grandfather fishes with the bright light of the sun out at sea where the fish are big and many."

"Your grandfather is older and weaker than anyone in the village," Kimo said, laughing. "Believe me, he sleeps in his boat and gets a fish from one of the young fishermen."

Makoa picked up a shell and tossed it out over the dark sea. It was true. His grandfather was old. His hands shook like palm fronds, and he couldn't even drag his canoe into the water without Makoa's help.

How could his grandfather possibly fish with the fiery sun?
That night, Makoa left the beach with a heavy heart.

The next morning, when Grandfather paddled to shore, Makoa was not there to greet him.

When grandfather got home, he said, "Makoa, I missed seeing you on the beach, waiting to welcome me home."

Makoa looked into Grandfather's sun washed eyes. "A boy told me you paddle to a nearby village to get your fish."

"Do you believe the boy?" Grandfather asked.

"I don't know what to believe," Makoa cried. "Can you bring me some proof that you truly fish with the sun?"

Grandfather slowly shook his head. "Sometimes you must believe in things you cannot see."

That afternoon, Makoa walked down to the beach with Grandfather. "Where are you going?" he asked.

"I am going torch fishing with the sun," Grandfather replied. "If I don't pull the sun from the sky and make it night, how will the torch fishermen catch any fish with their feeble flames?" Then he paddled away.

When it was dark, the torch fishermen came down to the beach. Kimo squatted next to Makoa and asked, "Where is your grandfather? Has he gone to the next village to get your fish?"

"No, he is torch fishing with the sun," Makoa replied.

"You really believe that?" Kimo asked.

Makoa nodded. "Sometimes you must believe in things you cannot see."

Kimo shook his head. "I only believe what I see," he said, laughing. "And I see that your grandfather is old and weak. He could not hold up a torch, never mind capture the sun!"

Makoa simply smiled, and the next morning he ran down to the beach to welcome Grandfather home.

And so the years passed, Makoa grew tall and strong.
And still, late every afternoon, he helped Grandfather push
his canoe onto the sea. And every morning, in the shell pink
dawn, he watched Grandfather paddle home.

The day finally came when Grandfather couldn't rise from his bed. Makoa knelt beside the old man and held his hand.

Grandfather smiled. "All these years you have believed that I fished with the sun as my torch," he said.

Makoa nodded.

"Now I leave you my canoe, my net, and my spear, for I am too old to paddle over the edge of the sea," Grandfather said weakly. And with a sigh as soft as a plumeria petal, he closed his eyes for the last time.

That evening, the sun did not slip over the edge of the sea the way it usually did, and night never came. The fishermen went down to the beach with their torches, but their feeble flames did not attract any fish while the sun still burned bright in the sky. The next day it was the same way. And the next, and the next. Soon the torch fishermen's families grew hungry.

Makoa knew he had to do something, so he took Grandfather's canoe and pushed it onto the water. He got in and paddled and paddled, his arms aching with every stroke.

When he got to the edge of the sea, he gathered the net in his arms and looked to the sky.

Makoa hesitated. How can I fish with the fierce sun? he wondered. Surely it will burn my net and fall down and burn me, too.

Then he remembered the many years Grandfather had said he torch fished with the sun, and very faintly he heard Kimo's taunting laughter still ringing in his ears.

Taking a deep breath, Makoa cast one end of his
net high into the sky. He watched as it spread wide
and smooth like a perfect seashell, before catching the
fierce sun like a hand catching a pebble. Makoa
laughed with joy as he tugged the sun over the edge of
the sea with him.

Holding the sun torch high to attract fish to his spear, Makoa knew Grandfather was with him. He felt him in his raw hands and sunburned shoulders and in the warm breeze and salty spray. Grandfather was there, even though he could not see him.

Now many giant fish surged around his canoe, attracted by his bright sun torch. Makoa took his time spearing one before he released the sun, and it was morning.

As Makoa paddled back to the island, he saw Kimo waiting for him on the beach. The canoe skimmed the shore and Kimo said, "Where did you go last night? The sky was dark again, and we caught many fish."

Makoa smiled. "I went over the edge of the sea," he said. "I went torch fishing with the sun."